RAINLAND

Sarah Allending

Rainland

SARAH
ALLERDING

Rainland – Rainland book 1

Copyright © 2016 Sarah Allerding

Cover by Perry Elisabeth Design | perryelisabethdesign.com

ISBN-13: 978-1535537520

ISBN-10: 1535537523

To my friend, whose encouragement pushed me to turn the results of a writing exercise into this book.

Acknowledgements:

I want to thank everyone who helped me make this story better including Nicole, my brother Matthew, my beta readers Claire and Faith, and several who wish to remain anonymous.

I also want to thank my Lord and Savior Jesus Christ for giving me my imagination and the ability to put that imagination on paper.

Chapter One

Eerie silence. Dark sky. Unbearable heat. Air as stagnant as the water at the bottom of a well. No substantial shelter within miles.

An ominous feeling welled up inside of Thomas. Something bad was going to happen and it was going to—

A loud crash tore through the humid night as if it were ripping a gigantic hole through the sky. Immediately, torrents of angry rain poured from the clouds like a river cascading over a rocky cliff. Thomas, who was completely drenched the minute the rain reached him, was knocked off his feet by the force of the water. He stared into the sky in utter horror. An angry black cloud was rapidly rotating above him. A tornado! Frantically, Thomas tried to get to his feet, but the torrential rain was too strong and he soon gave up. Squeezing his eyes shut as tightly as he could, Thomas braced himself for the impact. The agonizing wait, while no more than five seconds, seemed to last forever. With a tremendous roar, Thomas was sucked into the swirling wind. Where was he going to land? The spinning stopped. He had landed on something solid.

"That's not a cow!" screeched a high-pitched voice nearby.

"If it's not a cow, what is it?" asked a second voice.

Thomas sat up and opened his eyes. Everything was spinning around him. He shook himself, trying to get rid of his dizziness. "W-where am I?" he sputtered thickly.

"You've entered the world of rain by the mistake of our captain," grumbled the first voice, which he could now tell was coming from a rather large raindrop that was standing over him. "He thought you were a cow."

"I-I don't understand," Thomas replied, bewildered.

"Well, first of all, let me introduce myself," replied the first voice. "I am A Water. We are all raindrops. The captain is Captain H2O. Now, we all live in the clouds, but we do not have everything we need. When we need something, like a cow, we touch down on the ground and pick it up. Captain H2O thought you were a cow. That is why he directed us to pick you up."

Thomas, still in a daze, looked around to see what he could make of his surroundings. There was an entire city in the clouds inhabited by thousands upon thousands of raindrops. There were railings all along the borders of the cloud as a feeble attempt to keep the raindrops from falling out. The hard surface on which he had landed was made of mismatched boards, worn from years of constant use. He could see massive staircases spiraling downward in multiple places on the deck-like floor of the cloud. He assumed they must lead to some sort of basement. It would not make much sense to build a stairway that led to the open sky.

As of this morning, Thomas had not imagined that raindrops could talk, let alone build a city. Turning his head, Thomas focused his attention back on the raindrop who had spoken to him earlier. "Now that you know I am not a cow, how am I going to get back home?"

"You're not going home; not yet anyway," the captain stated matter-of-factly, stepping forward and placing his glasses on the tip of his nose. "We need you."

"W-what do you mean?" Thomas asked. Immediately, panic overwhelmed him as the realization hit him. He was trapped in an unknown world with absolutely no way out. He was helpless…at the mercy of an army of talking raindrops. He sank down with a groan of despair.

"Yes, yes!" A Water exclaimed, bouncing from foot to foot. Each time he bounced, ripples of water flowed from his head to his toes. Paying no attention to the boy's obvious distress at the captain's words, he went on, "You are the answer to all our problems! We will no longer have to contend with the lightning!"

"Calm down or you'll fall off the cloud and no one will be able to help you," Captain H2O barked. "Don't count your snowflakes until they have formed. This is the first time we have ever seen a human. We don't even know what he can do." Turning to Thomas he continued, "We have a very large predicament, you see. When our population density reaches a certain level, the lightning decides that some of us need to go. It then strikes us, sending torrents of us falling to the ground. Once this tragedy takes place, we lose our ability to talk and are completely at the mercy of the water cycle until we once again reach the clouds. That is, if we ever do. Some have never returned, and we suspect they are flowing along at the very bottom of some river or possibly even the ocean." At that he shivered.

Thomas sat up straight and stared at him. "So you're kidnapping me!" he practically shouted, jumping to his feet. "I've got to find a way to get home…" his voice trailed off. He scanned his surroundings. There was no way for him to escape apart from jumping over the edge of the cloud, which, of course, was a foolhardy thing to do since he was thousands of feet above the ground.

"It is a very foolish idea to try to get out of our kingdom, as you can no doubt see," remarked Captain H2O, polishing his glasses. Without looking up he went on, "You shall remain here until you have accomplished what no one has yet to accomplish for hundreds of years…" he lowered his voice to a menacing whisper, sending chills down Thomas' spine, "*defeat the lightning.*" With that he gave a stubborn smear on his glasses one last rub, and with an air of superiority, placed them back on the very tip of his nose.

Thomas stared at the captain in complete shock. Lightning? Defeat lightning? What did he know about lightning?

"A Water! See to it that this boy gets a room," the captain barked. With that, he turned on his heel, marched over to a room marked "Headquarters," and disappeared inside.

"Don't worry," A Water tried to assure Thomas. "He usually is quite easy to get along with. Follow me."

This was different. A Water was a raindrop. He was used to getting along with the captain.

Chapter Two

A Water led Thomas to one of the massive staircases. The stairs seemed to spiral on into endless blackness. Flaming torches lined the railing around the top of the stairway. A Water grabbed one and motioned for Thomas to do the same. As they made their way down the stairs, the light from their torches cast eerie shadows on the walls. Hundreds of drawings covered the stony walls. Stopping, Thomas held the torch up to a rather elaborate drawing of what looked like a massive castle. A raindrop with a crown could be seen seated on a stately horse with a long flowing mane. Wow! It was magnificent!

"King Fontaine the fifth," A Water whispered softly. "Used to be a great ruler. Kind and gentle from what I've heard." A dreamy look came over his face.

Thomas ran his hand over the drawing. "Where is he now?"

"Lightning got him," A Water replied with a dismal look in his eyes. The look on his face told Thomas that the loss of this king was a very tragic event in the history of Rainland. "The lightning hit his castle one day five hundred years ago. It hurled many raindrops from the clouds. He was one of them. Sadly, he never came back. Somewhere, in some lake or river, he is waiting to evaporate so he can return."

The rest of their descent was spent in silence as the two of them thought about the king. Their footsteps echoed through the stairwell with a hollow thudding sound. Upon reaching the last step, A Water lifted his torch and lit several other torches near the ceiling. Thomas looked in amazement at the massive corridors that seemed to go on forever.

"This is what is left of the castle," A Water explained, as they followed a narrow hallway lined with iron doors. "The lightning totally leveled the part above ground. That is why everything upstairs is rebuilt with a more modern touch." He stopped in front of a door marked, "Long awaited guest," and took out a strange looking key. He inserted the key in the lock and opened the door.

Thomas followed, his eyes glued to the sign on the door. What could that mean? Did they think he was someone special?

"Make yourself at home," A Water said. He stood on his tiptoes as he lighted the embers in the lantern that hung from the ceiling. The lantern was merely a metal bowl hung by four chains. A soft crackling sound filled the air as the flame spread throughout the bowl. "I'll be back in an hour with your supper." With that, A Water disappeared down the corridor in the direction they had come. Thomas listened as his footsteps faded into the distance.

Thomas looked around the small room. The walls were bare except for a portrait of a raindrop in a flowing red robe with a crown on its head. It had to be the long-lost king. A small cot made out of stone jutted out from the back wall. It looked very cold and uninviting. Who would want to sleep on a stone cot? Then, he remembered. This was designed for raindrops. Raindrops cannot lie on porous surfaces or they would soak right through. That must be why everything was made of either stone or metal! Lying down, Thomas decided to try to get a little rest before dinner. As he closed his eyes, he heard a faint rumble in the distance.

Thomas had no more than drifted off to sleep when a deafening screeching sound jarred him awake. Red lights were flashing through the corridor. "Get to safety!" A voice boomed. Hundreds of raindrops were running headlong down the staircases. Thomas got up and watched as they swarmed through the corridors, frantically searching for rooms in which to hide. One young raindrop ran into Thomas' room in a panic. "Help! Help!" he screamed, running into Thomas. His eyes grew big as he noticed that the object he ran into was a boy, "A m-m-MONSTER!" His eyes bugged out. He had obviously never seen a human before. Frozen in fear, his finger shook as he pointed at Thomas.

A large raindrop entered Thomas' room and grabbed the young raindrop's outstretched arm. "That is not a monster. Come on, we have to stay with our group. I don't want anyone lost," she said urgently. The little raindrop followed, his fearful eyes still glued on Thomas. The clatter of thousands of raindrops echoed throughout the corridors. What was going on? The last of the raindrops hurried past his door. After a few minutes had passed, A Water walked in, holding a giant ring of keys.

"I haven't forgotten your supper," he said in a weary voice. "It is cooking on an open fire upstairs. We are not to go up until we are sure the thunder has passed." That explained it. The raindrops were seeking shelter from a possible attack by the lightning. A shiver went down Thomas' spine. This was the lightning he was supposed to defeat.

"Do you take shelter every time you hear thunder?" Thomas asked, taking a seat on the stone cot.

A Water nodded. "If you hear thunder, you are close enough to be struck by lightning. It is a very terrifying thing when the lightning strikes. We have a lot of rooms down here where we attempt to hide." He lifted his ring of keys. "Four hundred rooms to be exact. We are not completely safe down here though. If the lightning really wants to, it can get us here, although it would be much harder."

Thomas and A Water sat in silence as they waited for the all clear. After what seemed like an hour, a buzzer went off. "We are now safe to return to ground level," a loud voice boomed over the speakers. Doors began opening up and down the halls as raindrops, eager to resume normal life, made their way to the staircases. "No, no, NO!" A terrified voice pleaded. "No MONSTER!"

"I told you before he is not a monster," replied another voice. "Come on, we have to get upstairs and finish supper. Don't you want to eat your supper? I know you are very fond of food."

"No, NO!" came the fearful reply. Thomas looked out to see the young raindrop who had run into him earlier. His feet were firmly planted and he was trying as hard as he could to pull away from the raindrop who held his hand. "Please, PLEASE!" he begged, nearly in tears.

"I won't hurt you," Thomas said softly, stepping out of his room and kneeling in order to make himself appear less intimidating. "I am a boy, not a monster. My name is Thomas, what is yours?"

"Drip," the young raindrop replied, relaxing a little.

"That's a nice name." Thomas smiled.

"Thank you," came the whispered reply.

"How about you help me prepare Thomas' supper?" A Water suggested.

Drip looked up questioningly at the raindrop who was holding his hand. His face was still clouded with apprehension. "Go ahead," she replied, relaxing her grip on his hand. "You love serving food."

A Water took Drip's hand and together they climbed the spiral staircase. "I'm Rain." The raindrop who had been with Drip extended her hand.

20

"It is nice to meet you," Thomas replied, shaking her hand. "I'm sorry I frightened Drip."

"That's okay, he is a naturally fearful droplet." She smiled at Thomas. "Well…it was nice meeting you. I really must be getting back to my cooking before it burns." With a wave of her hand, Rain disappeared up the winding staircase.

Chapter Three

As A Water and Drip entered the kitchen, Drip made a beeline for the cupboards, flinging them open with enthusiasm. He *loved* preparing meals. He proceeded to pull out all of his favorite foods and place them on the floor. "This will be fun!" he exclaimed, his head buried in the cupboard.

A Water, who was distracted by the potatoes that had been roasted over the fire, paid no attention to Drip. The fire had gone out during the evacuation and the potatoes were cold. Fumbling around, he found some matches and relit the fire. "There," he said to himself. "They should be just right in a few minutes." Turning around, he noticed the mountain of food on the floor. Drip was half in the cupboard. Every few seconds, a new item of food joined the growing pile.

"Drip, what *are* you doing? We are feeding a boy, not an army!"

Slowly, Drip emerged from the cupboard, his face covered in flour. He grinned up at A Water. "I want Thomas to try all my favorite foods!"

"That's very nice of you." A Water smiled back. "But Thomas' stomach isn't that big! Let's pick a few of your favorites and save the others for another day, okay?"

Drip looked at the food surrounding him. After thinking for a while he agreed. "Okay, as long as he gets to try all of it some time."

"Don't worry, he will." A Water got down on his hands and knees and began helping Drip put the excess food back in the cupboard. They saved the rolls, tomatoes, and a bar of chocolate to add to the potatoes they were going to give Thomas.

~~~

"Can I have the food yet?" came an impatient voice from the stairway. Thomas smiled to himself. It must be Drip. He sat down in preparation for his supper.

"I told you I would give it to you when we get down the stairs," A Water replied laughing. "I don't want you to drop it." Presently A Water appeared with Drip right behind him. Drip hesitated when he reached the door, remembering his fear of the boy. He looked up at A Water. "You're okay." A Water gave his shoulder a reassuring squeeze.

Drip cautiously crept over to the stone cot and set the plate of food down. Immediately, he retreated to the safety of the hall and peered into the room to watch Thomas. He had to know that Thomas liked his food.

Thomas took a bite of a tomato and smiled. "Mmmm…this is delicious!" He winked at Drip, eliciting a smile. Turning to A Water he asked, "What exactly is going to happen next?"

A Water sobered. "You are to meet with me and Captain H2O for a meeting. This will take place bright and early tomorrow morning. We need to discuss our plans for defeating the lightning."

Thomas' face clouded. "There must be some mistake. What do I know about lightning that you don't?

A Water looked surprised. "You are a human!" As if that explained everything. Thomas was more confused than ever. "Follow me!" A Water jumped up. Looking at Drip he said, "You better run along to bed. You need to get some sleep so you will be ready to prepare Thomas' breakfast. He is getting up bright and early."

That was all the incentive Drip needed. Before Thomas could blink, he had disappeared up the staircase.

A Water led Thomas down the hall. Turning a corner, they arrived in a large library. Shelves of old books lined the walls. Racks upon racks of ancient scrolls occupied the middle of the room. Each scroll had the name of a king stamped on the outside. They looked like they hadn't been touched in more than a century. The same kind of lantern that hung in Thomas' room lined the ceiling. A Water reached up and lit one with a match he had been carrying. "Have a seat," he gestured toward a stone chair. Pulling a large book from a shelf, he sat down at the table and leafed through the pages. The book was titled, "History of Eldur." "Here." A Water stabbed the page with his finger. "Read this."

Thomas looked at the page in shock. A picture of Benjamin Franklin with the words, "Man to be feared," jumped off the page. "This is the history book from our enemy," A Water explained. He turned around and grabbed a map off of a nearby table. "Here is Rainland, and here is Eldur." Thomas noticed a picture of a giant volcano with black smoke curling out of it. It had a sinister look to it which Thomas did not like. It gave him a creepy feeling inside. A Water went on, "Eldur is the source of all fire and the home of the lightning. It is ruled by a very cruel king by the name of Ignatius. His name means, 'Fiery one," and does he ever have a fiery temper! He does have a weakness, although he would never admit it. He is unable to survive in water. He and his subjects are flames. That is why he is friendly with the lightning. He wants to keep our population down so that we can't overpower him."

Thomas was horrified. He not only had to defeat the lightning, he was up against a sinister band of flames!

"But what does this have to do with Benjamin Franklin?" Thomas asked with a puzzled look.

"Because," A Water explained, pointing to the text, "He made some special rods that kept the lightning from striking houses. We thought, since you are a human, you could help us figure out how to keep the lightning away from us."

Thomas shook his head in bewilderment. "I don't know enough about that and that was done on the ground. This is a totally different world up here. I don't think it would work."

"No, I don't think that would work here either, and that is not what we want. We want the lightning defeated completely. There's got to be something you can do, "A Water said, attempting to hold back a yawn. "We had better get to bed or we won't be alert at the meeting in the morning. Meet us here at seven."

Chapter Four

What was that sound? It sounded like someone opening the ice box. A Water got out of bed to investigate. Walking into the kitchen, he was surprised to see Drip sitting at the table spreading jam on a piece of toast. He was getting more jam on himself than the piece of bread. At least he appeared to be enjoying himself. "Drip?"

Startled, Drip looked up with his sticky face. A Water could tell he had been eating some of the jam. "I am making breakfast for Thomas."

"When I said bright and early, I didn't mean this early." A Water chuckled. "It is only four in the morning! Here let's get you cleaned up. You have jam all over your face!"

When Drip's face was once again clean, he walked over to the table in order to resume his task of making breakfast. "Oh no you don't," A Water said with a smile. "Let's go back to bed and finish in the morning. Drip looked disappointed as A Water put the bread back in the ice box. "Don't worry, I will be sure to get you up in time."

~~~

Sleep didn't come easily for Thomas. He had too much on his mind. How was he ever going to solve this problem? He had to find a way. If he didn't, he would never get home. Finally, after a rather fitful night, Thomas decided to get dressed so he would be ready for breakfast. When he was ready, he opened his door so Drip would know he could come in. After a while, he heard soft tapping on the stairs. He smiled to himself. It must be Drip. Sure enough, Drip appeared with a plate full of toast with jam. Drip sat down in the doorway to wait. "Are you really going to get rid of the lightning?" he asked in a barely audible voice.

Thomas froze. What should he say? "I don't know, I guess I have to try or I'll never get home." There was a tinge of bitterness to his voice, which Drip picked up on.

"You don't like it here, do you?" Drip asked softly, sadness filling his brown eyes. "Are you sad?"

"Well…I…" Thomas didn't know what to say. He hadn't meant to disappoint the little raindrop.

Drip sighed. "I am an orphan because of the lightning. I need you."

Thomas stopped chewing. "I thought A Water and Rain…" he trailed off, an awful feeling welling up inside of him.

"They are my older brother and sister," Drip replied. "Will you please do something?" A small tear formed in Drip's eye and slowly made its way down his face and onto the floor. "Will they ever get to come back?"

Thomas was not expecting this. What could he say? "I will do my best, okay, Drip?"

Drip smiled and brushed away his tears. Without another word, he grabbed Thomas' empty plate and dashed up the stairs.

Thomas sat back against the wall. Now more than ever he wanted to defeat the lightning. How could anyone, even a sinister fire king, want to make a little raindrop so sad?

Thomas got up and made his way over to the library where A Water and Captain H2O were already seated around one of the stone tables. "Please take a seat," the captain said without even looking up. He was intently studying the map that A Water had shown Thomas the night before.

"So what are the plans you wanted to talk about?" Thomas asked, taking a seat.

"You are going to go to Eldur as a spy," Captain H2O replied matter-of-factly, peering over his glasses at Thomas.

"You can't be serious!" Panic threatened to overtake him.

"We've talked it over," A Water responded. "We want you to go into Eldur and gather as much information as you can. We need you to find out where in the land of Eldur the lightning resides. Once we figure that out, we can work on a plan to stop it once and for all. You are going to go in under the cover of darkness. If you are careful, you should not have any problems."

Thomas thought for a minute. "How would defeating the lightning help those who have been knocked to the ground?" The story Drip told him was on his mind and he wanted to find a way to help.

A Water grabbed a book called, "Laws of the Land," and opened to a page. "Right here it says that once the lightning is defeated, the power of the water cycle is weakened. Only those who wish to remain in the water cycle will remain. The rest will immediately evaporate and return to Rainland."

"When do we start and what preparations are to be made?" Thomas asked, eager to get this dangerous task over with.

"We will need to get to Eldur," A Water replied, getting up and placing the book back on the shelf. "Captain and I will set up council with the wind. I am sure it will be willing to take us."

Set up council with the wind? Talking raindrops were one thing, and talking flames another, but the wind? Thomas tried to imagine the wind sitting down at a table and talking but he just couldn't picture it.

"Meanwhile," A Water went on, "We will have a fireproof suit made for you. You shall go to the tailor's tomorrow to get fitted. We'll let you know what the wind says."

Thomas left the two raindrops to make their plans on getting in touch with the wind. He decided to rest since the days to come would be busy days.

Chapter Five

The next day was calm and clear. Thomas noticed the happy laughter of the droplets as they played. He was on his way to the tailor, which was located on the ground level. A group of droplets were playing tag next to the shop. He smiled when he saw that Drip was "it." With a wave of his hand, Thomas opened the door and disappeared into the shop. A raindrop with wire rimmed glasses approached him. "I'm Dover. I have been expecting you. Let's get going on your suit. You will be needing it any day now." After a few quick measurements, Dover disappeared into the back room. Thomas looked around at the different garments that were either being sold or repaired. All the clothing was waterproof. That made sense to

Thomas. Raindrops were wet and would not want to have their clothes soaked.

After about a half an hour had passed, Dover emerged from the back room with the finished suit. "Here, try it on," he said, giving it to Thomas.

Thomas pulled it on over his clothes. It was a light brown color so he could blend in with the brown landscape of Eldur. He had never seen material like this before. It must be an invention of Rainland. "Looks good."

Dover nodded with satisfaction. "A Water said to meet him and the captain at the headquarters on your way back. Something about the wind." He disappeared into the back room, leaving Thomas to himself.

After making sure his new clothes were folded neatly, Thomas made his way to headquarters. He barely stepped inside when A Water began talking, "The wind said yes. It is going to start blowing us tonight!" His face showed his excitement at the prospect that their struggle with the lightning might at long last be nearing its end. "All of Rainland will be traveling to the mouth of Eldur. It should take about twenty-four hours to get there."

Good, Thomas thought. He could use the extra time to prepare himself mentally. "Is there anything I should do in the meantime?"

"We will go over everything tomorrow," A Water replied. "Now, you should get some rest before lunch. Drip has something special up his sleeve." He winked.

～

"Thomas, Thomas, open the door!" Thomas sat up. He must have been sleeping for a while. Rising, he went to open the door. Drip could hardly contain his excitement. "I have my favorite dish for you!"

Thomas eyed him with a suspicious twinkle in his eyes. "I thought everything was your favorite."

"Well, this is my favorite of my favorites!" Drip exclaimed, causing Thomas to laugh. Drip pulled the lid off with a dramatic flourish. "Cucumber broccoli lasagna with fish sauce!" he announced triumphantly.

Smiling, Thomas winced inwardly. The combination did not sound very appealing. "That must have taken you a while to make." Thomas took the plate from Drip's outstretched hand.

"An entire hour." Drip beamed proudly.

Thomas sat down and cut a corner from the lasagna. The juicy sauce dripped out from between the layers. "This is really good!" Thomas exclaimed after swallowing his first bite.

Chapter Six

"Now for the planning." A Water sat down next to Thomas. They were once again gathered in the library to go over the plans. The wind had kept its word and all of Rainland was on its way to the mouth of Eldur. "We will reach Eldur just after dark. You will be lowered down with a rope. There will be flames guarding the mouth of the volcano. It is very important that no one sees you. If they do, it could mean the end for all of us." There was an edge to A Water's voice that sent chills down Thomas' spine. What was he getting into?

Thomas shifted to the edge of his seat and planted his elbows on the table. "What happens if they catch me?"

In answer, A Water grabbed the history book of Eldur and opened to a page titled, "humans." Pushing it across the table, he pointed to a drawing at the bottom of the page. Thomas' eyes grew wide. There was a sketch of a person locked in a dungeon with the caption, "Any human we find must be captured." A heavy silence hung over the room as the realization hit Thomas. If he were caught, he would never get home.

Thomas slid back in his chair and ran his fingers through his hair. "Why can't one of you go?"

"Like I said before," A Water replied, patiently, "Once any of us leave the clouds, we are no longer able to speak, walk, or do anything except what the water cycle tells us to do. You can do it Thomas. We know you can." Thomas wished he had as much confidence as A Water had in him. "We need you to get as much information as you can."

"I'll try." Thomas rose. "I think I would like to get some sleep before we get there."

~~~

Thomas opened his eyes with a start. Someone was knocking on his door. "It is time," came a whisper.

Thomas' stomach turned in knots at the prospect of his dangerous mission. Getting up, he opened his door. There stood A Water and Drip. Tears were streaming down Drip's face. Thomas knew that he needed to be strong for Drip.

"Don't get caught please," Drip begged in a choked voice. He had grown quite fond of the boy and did not want anything to happen to him.

"Don't worry." Thomas tried to sound reassuring, but he could not easily hide his nervousness. "I will be careful." He gave Drip a wan smile.

"Get your fireproof suit on. We don't have any time to lose," A Water said. His impatience leaked through his tone of voice even though Thomas could tell he was trying hard not to let it show. "We are almost there."

Thomas pulled his suit on and followed A Water up the staircase. The upper level was deserted. Most of the raindrops had been evacuated to the lower level in case of an attack by the lightning. Only A Water, Captain H2O and Drip would be present for Thomas' descent into Eldur.

"There is Eldur." A Water pointed over the edge of the cloud. Eldur was one of several small islands that dotted the waters below. The edge of Rainland was directly above the edge of the volcano. Ominous black smoke billowed out of the volcano. Thick fiery lava boiled just below the surface. Its eerie glow emanated from the volcano, causing Thomas to feel like he was living in a vivid nightmare. He had never seen anything so intimidating in his entire life. Sure enough, little flames patrolled the edge of the volcano. Thomas could count four of them pacing back and forth. How could he get past them? Light shone all around them. If he got in their light, he would be caught for sure.

"It's time," A Water whispered, pointing to the rope.

Thomas nodded. Looking toward Drip, a lump formed in his throat. Would he be able to help? Would he ever see Drip again? Reaching out, he hugged Drip. Tears threatened to fill his eyes. Turning away, he began his decent down the rope, away from the safety of Rainland and into the unknown and dangerous world of Eldur.

Every inch brought Thomas closer to the dreadful task that lay ahead of him. The unbearable heat that rose from the volcano threatened to suffocate him. Looking down, he felt dizzy. His palms grew sweaty at the thought of falling, making him doubt his ability to hang on. There were no footholds, so he had to rely on his strength to keep from sliding down the rope. Was he even strong enough to climb back up? This was no time to think such thoughts. Taking a deep breath, he resumed his painful descent into the unknown.

At long last he reached the end of the rope. Looking around, he noticed that the guards had their backs turned to him. Now he would have to jump and find a safe hiding place so he could gather his thoughts.

He landed with a soft thud on the parched land. The impact caused him to land on his knees. The intensifying heat caused his head to pound. It felt as though he had crawled into an oven. He couldn't imagine how much worse it must be inside the volcano. Scrambling to his feet, he searched for a place to hide. The guards would surely be making their way back soon and he didn't want to be caught in the open when they did. Spotting a rock, he made a dash for it, concealing himself just as one of the guards turned to make his way back toward him. Thomas' heart pounded as he let out a sigh of relief. He had made it so far without detection. Now, to figure out where the lightning lived. He couldn't even begin to imagine how he would figure that out.

Chapter Seven

"No, no!" Drip protested as A Water led him down the stairs. "I want to see Thomas!"

"It is too dangerous to stay up there," A Water explained patiently. "If the lightning attacks, I don't want you to get hurt." They arrived at the door to a crowded room. Rain came out and took Drip's hand. "Please see if you can distract him," A Water said with a worried tone. "He is desperately afraid something will happen to Thomas."

Rain nodded, a look of understanding on her face. "Come on, Drip." She gave him a kind smile. "Why don't we make some lunch?"

"Not hungry," Drip croaked, slumping into a corner. He pulled his knees up to his chin and began rocking as a way to get rid of his nervous energy.

Rain turned and gave A Water a concerned look. He nodded, knowingly. There was nothing either of them could do about the situation.

~~~

From the safety of the rock, Thomas scanned the area, looking for anything that might give him a clue as to the whereabouts of the lightning. The only abnormal thing he could find was a large cylindrical object sticking out of the edge of the volcano's rim. He shifted his gaze to the nearest guard. He was almost at the point where he would turn and head away from Thomas. This was his chance. As much as he didn't want to, Thomas prepared himself to investigate the object. This might be his only lead and he had to check it out. As soon as the guard turned, Thomas crept out from behind the protection of the rock. He felt so exposed standing out in the open. Thankfully, he was under the cover of darkness. Keeping his eyes glued to the back of the guard, he made his way to the cylinder. The cylinder looked like an ordinary tube that might be found at a construction site. What exactly was this doing on the edge of a volcano? Thomas peered inside. The sight that met his eyes shocked him. Hundreds of small lightning bolts were walking around in a dungeon-like chamber! They had faces, hands, and feet just like the flames and raindrops! Thomas had not expected this. But then, he hadn't even expected the raindrops to act like people either.

"Who's tampering with our hole?" growled a menacing voice. Thomas jumped. Had one of the lightning bolts just spoken to him? Did it know he was there? Fear gripped his heart. Scrambling to get away, Thomas slipped on some rocks, sending them down into the volcano. The sound they made was deafening in the silent night air. Thomas laid flat, hoping he could escape detection. Holding his breath, he listened for any signs that anyone had heard the noise.

"What was that?" came a gruff voice nearby. Thomas turned his head and froze. Not more than four feet away stood one of the fire guards. He stood between Thomas and the rope that hung from Rainland, cutting off any hope that he could make it back. If the guard came any closer he would be sure to see Thomas.

"What's up, Fiery?" barked one of the other guards, turning around to see what had caused alarm. He made his way toward Thomas. The look on his face was anything but pleasant. Thomas guessed it was the result of years of such work. He definitely would not feel very pleasant working for such an evil king.

"I heard something," replied the first guard, stepping closer to where Thomas lay. Thomas had no idea how he could not notice him. He had practically stepped on him before stopping to answer his companion. The guard looked more intimidating as he towered over Thomas. "I think someone is here," the first guard went on. "I heard stones fall into the volcano and *I'm* not the one who dislodged them." He lowered his eyes until they landed on Thomas' shoe. "What is *that?*" He lifted his gaze until it rested on Thomas' face. Thomas felt as though the guard's eyes were boring holes through him.

The second guard followed his gaze. His eyes grew large and his mouth dropped open in shock. "It's a *human!* His majesty's most fearsome enemy!" Thomas scrambled to his feet in a wild attempt to get away. "After him! We can't let him get away!"

Reaching the rock, Thomas stopped for a moment to catch his breath. He eyed the rope hanging from the clouds. It was only a few yards away but under the circumstances, those few yards seemed like miles. "We've got him now!" one of the guards shouted as they came around the rock. Thomas looked from them to the rope and back again. This was his only chance. He made a break for it. "Stop him!" With a burst of energy, Thomas tore across the ground. When he was only a few feet away from the rope he looked back. The guards were quickly closing in on him. Catching his toe on a stone, Thomas lost his balance and fell down hard. He struggled to get up as one of the guards reached out to grab him. Rising to his feet, he jumped and grasped the end of the rope, just as the guards reached out and took hold of his feet.

~~~

"Something happened to him," Drip sobbed, now pacing the floor.

"Drip, we don't know that," Rain said in a soft voice. "For all we know, he could be coming back right now. Why don't you make some food for him? He will be starving!"

"I guess." Drip sounded very unenthused. He walked over the boxes that had been packed with food for their evacuation. Boxes of all shapes and sizes had been piled along the walls in each room where raindrops were staying. Drip lifted the flap on the one labeled, "tomatoes." Listlessly, he pulled a tomato out and placed it on the next box and began cutting it.

A Water entered the room with a determined look on his face. "Captain and I are going up. We can't stand the suspense."

Drip jumped up from his half-sliced tomato. "I'm going too!"

"No you stay here. I know you want to see how Thomas is, but you won't help him by getting hurt. He would want you to be safe." Rain gave him an understanding smile. "Here, let me help you make a meal for Thomas. Oh that is a great choice! Tomatoes!" She picked up the tomato that Drip had been slicing. "How about adding some lettuce, cucumbers, and croutons for a nice salad?"

A smile threatened to appear on Drip's face. "Okay."

A Water and Captain H2O grabbed a couple torches and made their way up the stairs.

"I don't like the silence up here," Captain H2O remarked as they reached the upper level. "It's eerie."

A Water nodded in agreement. "I hope Thomas is having success. I sure would hate for him to be captured."

"Send for the lightning!" came a cry from below the clouds.

"What was that?" A Water paled. It looked like he had seen a ghost. A look of utter horror spread across his face.

"*Thomas!*" The captain ran toward the edge where they had tied the rope. A Water wasn't far behind. They ran faster than any raindrop had ever been known to run. The sight that met their eyes caused their stomachs to turn in knots. Thomas was barely hanging on to the end of the rope. A flame, one of the guards they guessed, was holding onto his feet. Another flame was running at breakneck speed in the direction of the volcano.

With a final burst of energy, Thomas freed his feet from the guard's hands and, with strength he didn't know he had, scurried up the rope.

"The lightning," Thomas gasped, collapsing at the captain's feet. "They are sending the lightning after me!" A deafening roar blasted from the volcano, shooting hundreds of lightning bolts directly at Rainland. The lightning looked like fireworks shooting into the sky before they explode. Under any other circumstance, Thomas would have enjoyed the sight, but it only brought more terror.

"Get to cover!" the captain shouted, pulling A Water behind a stone wall. The lightning hit with such force, it sounded like bombs were exploding everywhere.

Thomas looked up as buildings were demolished. Broken rock was flying through the air. How was he going to get out of here? He had to get to safety. A large piece of a roof whizzed over his head and landed with a loud bang on the ground, shattering into a million pieces. One piece reminded him of pictures he had seen of shields that knights used to take into battle. Reaching over, he grabbed the edge. It was too heavy. He would have to get up so he could take it in both hands. Looking over his shoulder, Thomas waited for a break in the volley of debris from the buildings. Here was his chance. Pulling himself to his knees, Thomas closed his fingers around the edge of the stone. Another deafening blast, accompanied by the sound of exploding buildings, sounded through the night air. The lightning was back for a second round. Thomas lifted the stone just as a bolt of lightning was about to strike him. It struck the stone shield with such force that Thomas was knocked flat on his back. Surprisingly, the shield didn't break. Pushing himself up, Thomas stood, holding the shield in front of his face in case another strike came his way.

"I want to help," came A Water's voice, as a jagged stone whistled by, narrowly missing his head.

Thomas had been so agitated by the lightning, that he hadn't noticed when A Water joined him. "Get in the basement!" Thomas shouted above the noise. "Drip needs you! He doesn't need to lose anyone else."

Reaching out from behind the wall, which surprisingly was still intact, the captain grabbed A Water's arm and pulled him to safety, just as another lightning bolt headed for Thomas. It struck with violent force, shattering the shield. The impact hurled Thomas from the clouds. "Ahhhhhhhhhhhhhhhhhhh!" The echo of Thomas' voice reverberated through the night sky as he plummeted toward the water below. Where was he going to land?

Chapter Eight

Thomas opened his eyes. Where was he? He hadn't remembered seeing any brick walls in Rainland. Then he remembered the battle with the lightning. The last thing he remembered was falling off the cloud. How did he get here? To his right, he noticed a large door made of strong iron bars. The air was cold and damp and smelled charred. He must have been captured by the flames once he had landed. Looking down, he noticed that his hands and feet were tied with sturdy rope. A large sigh came from behind him. "They tie really tightly. I doubt you'll get them off."

Who had just spoken to him? Thomas craned his neck as far as he could. Being bound limited his mobility considerably. He gasped at the sight that met his eyes. He was in the same chamber he had looked into from above. The chamber was full of lightning bolts. The same lightning bolts that had just tried to destroy Rainland. His face darkened. "So, you got your wish. What are you going to do with me now?" His voice was tinged with bitterness.

"Well." The lightning bolt who had spoken earlier got up and stood in front of Thomas. "If we could, we'd untie your hands and feet." Thomas looked at him. He wasn't sure if he was trying to mock him or if in fact he was serious. "Really, I mean it. We all would be glad to help you." The lightning bolt took Thomas by the shoulders and turned him around so he could rest his back against the wall. "We're all sorry about the attack last night, and especially about knocking you off the clouds." The rest of the lightning bolts nodded in agreement.

"My name is Donder," the lightning bolt went on. "We are captives of the flame who calls himself king. We are stuck in this dungeon. We have no choice but to attack anything and everything that the king commands." Donder rejoined the rest of the lightning bolts and waited for Thomas to respond.

Thomas thought for a while. Donder did seem to be sincere, but it was still too hard to believe. He had been sent on this mission specifically to defeat the lightning. Now he was hearing that the lightning didn't really want to attack. He would need time to sort all this out. What about everything he had heard from the Captain and A Water? It was written in the history books. "But the history books." Thomas looked at Donder.

"Ahh, the lies." A look of disgust formed on Donder's face. "His 'Majesty' King Ignatius, wrote those books. A long time ago he got hold of the real text books from Rainland and Eldur and had them burned. You see, he wants power. If he can get his subjects to believe lies, he can control them more easily. He makes them think what he wants them to think. But," he lowered his voice to a nearly inaudible whisper. "We lightning bolts hid one of the original copies of the true history of Eldur. It is safely locked away where none of the flames will ever find it."

"What is the true history of Eldur?" Thomas questioned. He was now very interested in this unexpected turn of events. Wiggling, he scrunched closer to the lightning bolt in order to hear better.

Still whispering, Donder continued, "You see, hundreds of years ago, Eldur belonged to the lightning. One tragic day, a ship ran aground on our shores and burned. Some of the flames made their way to our land. Once they were here, they had the ability to talk, walk, and act like humans, something they had never been able to do before. In fact, this is the only place in the whole world where they can do such things. Relishing these newfound abilities, they invaded our land. They were filled with greed and wanted nothing but complete power and control. They hurt anyone in their way. We were made slaves; tools to do their evil deeds. Mostly, they used us to keep the population of Rainland down in order to make sure they remained powerful."

Thomas looked down the hall leading away from the dungeon, making sure no one was listening. "Where is this history book hidden?"

"Ahh," Donder folded his arms. "There is a secret tunnel that leads out of the volcano. The flames do not know about it. There is a key that opens this tunnel. Inside the tunnel, a copy of the original history of Eldur is hidden in a crevice. This crevice is well hidden so it is doubly protected from those who would like to have it destroyed. If you can get out of here and get the key, we could all get out of here."

Thomas looked at him in shock. "How would I get out of here? There are hundreds of you and you haven't gotten out."

"Don't know really," Donder sighed. He slumped down. Thomas looked around at the rest of the lightning bolts. They all looked like they thought existence was the most painful experience they had ever been through. How he longed to help them once again enjoy life. But how? How could he get out and accomplish such a task? He was, after all, only a boy.

Chapter Nine

A Water jolted awake as the first rays of sunlight peaked over the horizon. The sky was splashed with a rosy hue. They beauty of it was spoiled by the events of the night. A Water shivered at the memory of Thomas hurtling over the edge of the cloud. He could not erase the scream from his memory. It played over and over, threatening to make him mad. "Captain! I'm going to check on Drip." The captain mumbled something unintelligible, which A Water took as his agreement.

Once downstairs, A Water noticed how tired he was. He must not have slept for more than an hour. The battle had taken up much of the night. He sighed. Hopefully this was not a failed mission. Reaching the door to the room Drip was in, he rested his hand on the door knob. Hopefully Drip had gotten some sleep. He had been very distressed about Thomas. A Water hated to see him that way. How was he going to explain what happened last night?

Rain put a finger to her lips as A Water entered. Drip was sleeping on the box of tomatoes, still clutching a half-sliced tomato. Finally, exhaustion had taken control over his fears, driving him to a sound sleep. Rain and A Water stepped into the hall so they could talk without the risk of waking Drip. "What happened last night?" Rain asked, apprehensively. "It sounded awful!"

A Water sighed. Running his hand through his hair, he began to recount the events of the previous night. "The last we saw, the flames had captured Thomas. Who knows what they did or are doing to him," he finished.

Rain's eyes grew large as a gasp escaped from her throat. "This is horrible! What shall we do?"

"There is nothing we can do but wait." A Water slumped his shoulders against the cold wall and shook his head with sadness.

~~~

Footsteps could be heard in the hall outside the dungeon. Thomas looked up to see one of the fire guards with a basket. It must be feeding time. Thomas' stomach grumbled. It had been a long time since he had eaten anything. Taking a key out of his pocket, the flame unlatched the iron door and pushed it open. None of the lightning bolts looked even remotely interested in the prospect of food. Thomas soon understood why. Each of them was given a dark crusty piece of bread the size of his fist. Thomas almost choked on the pungent smell of charred bread. They must have thrown all the prisoners' bread in the lava chamber. It was as hard as a rock. As hard as he tried, Thomas could not even make a dent with his teeth. The fire guard looked at him like he was crazy to even try eating it. Why they bothered to bring this food, Thomas didn't know. The lightning bolts knew better than to even touch the stuff, leaving it where the guard had left it.

Placing his hands on his hips, the guard gave Thomas a piercing glare. "I'll be back for you. His majesty has requested your presence." Sneering, he turned, and pulled the heavy door shut. The sound of his receding footsteps grew quieter and quieter. The silence that followed was menacing. Thomas thought about the guard's words. What might the king do to him? His heart lurched at the thought.

Donder cleared his throat. "You must remember to address him as, 'Your Majesty.' If you don't, he will throw you into the lava." His words hung in the air, causing Thomas' spine to tingle. This king did not sound at all pleasant. No wonder his guards were so cold and heartless.

It wasn't long before the guard was back. Thomas thought he might untie his hands, but he only untied his feet. Standing up, he wobbled on his stiff legs. The rope had been tied rather tightly and his legs were weak from poor circulation. Unconcerned with his condition, the guard grabbed him roughly, and forcibly led him out through the door. Every few feet Thomas stumbled. The guard, having not the slightest bit of patience, dragged him on without slowing in the least.

The throne room was gigantic. It was hewn out of the rock in the volcano's wall. The ceiling rose more than three stories high. The throne was much larger than the king would ever need it to be. Thomas guessed that it made him feel more important to sit in an oversized throne. In his opinion, it only made him look ridiculous. The king and the queen, who sat on a much smaller throne at his left, were dressed in flowing yellow robes made of the finest fireproof fabric. "Eldurian Royalty," was stitched in bright gold across the front. "Kneel," the guard hissed through clenched teeth. "Don't you know how to behave?"

Thomas jumped. He noticed the guard on his knee, with a hand still securely holding the rope that was around his hands. The king's piercing stare communicated his disapproval of Thomas' behavior. Shaking, Thomas reluctantly dropped to a knee. "Y-your M-majesty," he stuttered.

The king seemed satisfied and Thomas silently let out his breath in relief. "What were you doing with the rain?" the king asked, coldly. He eyed Thomas with a look of complete hostility.

"They accidentally picked me up with a tornado," Thomas answered. The guard elbowed him in his ribs and glared at him. "Your majesty," Thomas added, dropping his eyes to the floor and trembling. The king seemed on the verge of losing what little patience he appeared to have.

"You will look at *ME* when I speak to you!" the king thundered.

Thomas lifted his head, wishing he was anywhere but here. The dungeon was wonderful compared to standing in the presence of the evil fire king.

"Better." The king gave a false smile. Attempting to sound kinder, he leaned forward and went on. "You have nothing to fear if you do as I say. You will find a way to get rid of the rest of the raindrops. Once you do, I will make you governor of Eldur. You will only have to answer to me." The sly look on his face betrayed his intentions. Thomas knew the king wouldn't hold his end of the deal if he were to do as he asked. Not that he would if the king were to keep his word. Thomas would never do anything to hurt the raindrops, no matter what the consequences were. "Take him back to the dungeon to think about my proposal," the king commanded the guard. "I shall send for him tomorrow afternoon."

The guard returned Thomas to the dungeon where he proceeded to retie Thomas' feet. When he was gone, Thomas began thinking about getting out. How could he do it? Looking down, the reminder of the tightly tied ropes on his hands and feet dashed his hopes. "We have to get out," he whispered to Donder who appeared to only be half asleep. "They want me to destroy the rest of Rainland."

"The key," Donder whispered. "The special key. We must get ahold of it. It is our only chance. It is the key that Benjamin Franklin used when he was experimenting with the lightning and his kite. This key will unlock our freedom. It will open the tunnel that contains our history book. If we can get that far, we can get out of this volcano. The flames fear the key because the man who 'tamed' lightning used it. They fear humans. That is why they don't like you. You are a threat to their power. If you were to make something like Benjamin Franklin, that diverted lightning away from houses, you could ruin their way to control the population of the rain."

"But how do I get the key?" Thomas questioned. "I am tied and there doesn't seem to be a way out of here." Looking around, his eyes fell on a jagged rock that had been used in the wall along the edge of the door. An idea popped into his head. He squirmed over toward the rock. This might work. It would have to work. He, the lightning, and the raindrops depended on him. Lifting his arms to the rock, he began working the rope back and forth over the sharp edge. One by one, the threads began to break. There was a lot of rope to work through, but he was confident that with time, his arms would be free.

Noticing what he was doing, Donder smiled. "That is brilliant!"

After a lot of rubbing on the rock, Thomas was able to break the rope the rest of the way. Reaching down, he attempted to untie his feet. The knot was stubborn. It didn't help that his fingers were stiff. Slowly, the knot loosened. With a final tug Thomas smiled. "I'm free."

Looking around, Thomas' smile turned into a frown. Now that his hands and feet were free, how would he get out of the dungeon? The iron door was securely attached to the brick walls. Thomas was about to slump down in despair when his eye caught something. The mortar around one of the bricks looked different. Could it be loose? Reaching up, he poked the brick with his finger. It moved! His heart skipped a beat. Maybe he was onto something. "Donder," he whispered.

Donder looked up at the sound of his name. "What is it?" His eyes grew large. "Thomas. You got your ropes off!"

Thomas nodded. "Yes and I need you to boost me up so I can better reach this brick. It's loose!" He could hardly contain his excitement. There was a chance they could get out. It wasn't much of a chance, not yet anyway, but it was more of a chance than they had ever hoped to have.

Once Donder had him high enough that he could really reach the brick, he began pushing on it with all his might. The mortar surrounding the brick began to crumble. Thomas stopped. What if the guard was nearby? Would he hear what he was doing and come to investigate? Could he possibly even be watching right now, waiting for Thomas to break free, only to capture him and tie him again? Maybe he would even put him in solitary confinement.

"What's the matter?" Donder questioned. "Isn't it working?"

"The guard," Thomas breathed.

Donder slowly let Thomas down and walked over to the door. Thomas joined him. There was no sign of the guard. Where could he be? Something moved in the far end of the corridor. A loud snore shattered the silence, indicating that the guard had fallen asleep. Thomas let out a sigh of relief. They had not been detected. Climbing back onto Donder's shoulders, he resumed the task of wiggling the lose brick. As the brick came free, Thomas pushed it in a way that it would not fall to the ground. He did not want to risk waking the guard with the noise it was sure to cause. Grabbing the end that stuck out, he pulled. Much to his delight, the bricks surrounding the one he had loosened were starting to break away from the rest. Carefully, he pulled them out, one by one and handed them down to Donder. The hole was now large enough for him to squeeze through. Thomas turned and looked at Donder. "I need you to put me through feet first."

Donder nodded and lifted him until his feet reached the edge of the hole. Thomas stuck his legs through and grabbed the edge of the hole. Once he was outside, he looked around. The guard was still sound asleep. The noise from his snoring had covered up any of the sounds that Thomas had made. Now that he was outside the dungeon, where should he go? How could he reach the secret tunnel? The key! He had to get Benjamin Franklin's key! But where was the key? "Where's the special key?" he whispered to Donder through the bars.

"In the armory," came the soft reply. "It is down the hall. You should not miss it. Be careful, there may be more guards."

A shiver went down Thomas' spine. He had gotten out of the dungeon, but he was not really free. He would not be free until he was out of this awful volcano where danger lurked around every corner.

Chapter Ten

After walking down the tunnel for what seemed like hours, Thomas encountered a large room carved out of the wall. This must be the armory. Inside, Thomas could see hundreds of suits of armor. No swords were in sight. Why wouldn't there be swords in an armory? Of course. How could he have forgotten the lightning? The flames didn't need any other weapons when they had the lightning on their side. Thomas scanned the area looking for guards. He felt like the suits of armor were looking at him. Where were all the guards?

Now to find the key. Thomas entered the armory. The key could be anywhere in this large room. How was he going to find it before the guards found out that he had escaped? They were sure to find out at breakfast time. He began making his way around the room, looking under and behind every piece of armor.

When he had made it half-way across the room, he stopped. What was that? Footsteps! Someone was coming! Thomas looked around wildly as the footsteps drew nearer. Where could he hide? His eyes rested on a small trunk. Dashing over, he lifted the trunk and climbed inside. Lowering the lid, he peered out.

"We'll need to feed the prisoners soon," came a deep voice.

"It's your turn to do that today," replied another. Thomas' eyes widened as two flame guards entered the room and made their way directly toward the trunk.

"You always leave me with the dirty work!" The first flame's voice was tinged with disgust. "I hate seeing the prisoners so miserable!"

"That is precisely why His Majesty wants you to do it. You must learn where your loyalties lie. You are to be loyal to the king and no other." The second flame gave him a disapproving look. "You'd better be careful. Your attitude risks the charge of treason. Now, where did I put my boots?" He reached for the lid of the trunk.

Thomas clamped a hand over his mouth in an attempt to stifle a gasp. He squeezed his eyes shut. They were sure to find him now.

A shout rang out through the hall. Thomas opened his eyes to see the flame guards turn from the trunk and race into the hall. His escape had been discovered! What might they do to the lightning bolts?

"How long do you think he has been gone?" asked one of the guards.

"Not sure," came the reply. "The lightning won't tell me anything."

Thomas decided to make a break for it before the guard came back for his boots. He figured he most likely had forgotten about them, but it would be best if he got out just in case. As he climbed out of the trunk, he noticed a small bump under the cloth that covered the bottom of the trunk. Could that be the key? The soft red cloth was stapled into the wood. Grabbing the small edge of the cloth, he tugged, trying to rip it free.

"Let's split up," came a voice outside. "It will be easier to find him that way. You take the armory. That would be a logical place for him to hide."

Thomas froze in mid-tear. They would find him now. He gave one last tug, ripping the cloth half-way off the bottom of the trunk. A feeling of disappointment surged through him. It was a piece of chewing gum! Why flames would have gum he didn't know, but what he did know was that he had to get out of there, and fast! Footsteps grew closer and closer. The guard assigned to search the armory would soon find him if he didn't find a place to hide. He looked wildly around before dashing across the room and concealing himself behind the largest suit of armor. They were full body suits on stands. It was easy for Thomas to stand up behind it and still be completely hidden from the entrance of the armory. The question was, how would he stay hidden if the flame came all the way into the back of the room? Hopefully he would give up before getting that far.

Thomas watched as the flame entered. Noticing the open trunk, he went over to investigate. Thomas winced. He should have thought to close the lid. Now the flame would know he was here, or at least know that he had been over there. The flame was right in line with Thomas' hiding place. If he turned, he was sure to see Thomas. Thomas tried to get on the other side of the armor and out of sight. In the process, his arm hit the edge of the armor, causing it to totter. Thomas held his breath hoping it would not fall.

A tremendous crash echoed through the room as the suit crashed into the next one. Much to Thomas' dismay, it didn't stop there. Each suit crashed into the one after it in a domino effect until the entire line had fallen. The flame spun around at the sound and gaped at the sight. Thomas got up and made a break for it.

"Oh, no you don't!" the guard called after him. Hurtling the fallen armor, he dashed after Thomas.

Thomas had no idea where he was going. His primary goal was to keep out of the flame's reach. Beginning to get tired, he turned to look behind him. The flame was still going strong, a look of determination on his face. The distance between them was rapidly closing as Thomas slowed out of weariness. The lack of substantial nutrition was taking its toll on him. How he wished he had forced himself to eat the horrible crusty bread. At least it would have helped, if only a little. Thomas felt like he was going in slow motion as his strength continued to grow weaker and weaker.

"Just give up. You know you can't outrun me." The flame was almost on top of him now.

Thomas stumbled, falling flat on his face. Struggling to get up, he noticed the shadow of the guard move over him. This was it. He was only able to rise as far as his knees when he felt the guard's strong grip on his shoulder.

Chapter Eleven

"I just don't know what to do." A Water paced back and forth. What were they going to do? It had been over a day and they had no way of knowing what had happened after Thomas had been captured. What might they do to him?

"Pacing won't bring him back," Captain H20 remarked curtly, looking up from the table. They were having an emergency meeting regarding Thomas.

"I know." A Water sank down in his chair and placed his hands over his eyes. He felt so hopeless. If only the captain could be a little more sympathetic, but it was his nature to approach everything in a business-like fashion. Growing more agitated, A Water again rose from the table to resume his pacing.

Their plans had gone so wrong. Why had Thomas been captured?

"If you can't sit still, I will not be able to concentrate." The captain gave A Water a piercing stare. "You are quite distracting."

"Sorry, I'll try to settle down." A Water slipped once again into the chair, this time determined not to leave it until their discussion was finished. "Is there anything you can find in the history book of Eldur?"

"Patience!" Captain H20 scowled. "I am still in the process of looking."

A Water watched as he flipped through the pages of the massive book. If he remembered correctly, most of the pages were filled with worthless information recounting the flame kings' evil achievements. Nothing of much use to them at this time. Sighing, he rested his chin in his hands.

"Ahh." The captain adjusted his glasses and pointed to the page. "This talks about what they will do to humans if they ever find one."

A Water gasped. This was the important information they had been searching for, but now he wasn't sure he wanted to know it. Knowing how evil the flames were, he knew that their plans for humans would most likely include cruelty.

"Humph," the captain remarked, looking intently at the page. "It says they will take any humans captive and force them to assist them in…" His voice quieted to a hoarse whisper. "Wiping out the entire population of raindrops." He stopped there and stared at A Water.

A chill slowly prickled down A Water's spine. A cold dreadful feeling washed over him. They were going to try to force Thomas to destroy Rainland. "Would he do it?"

The captain leaned back in his chair and folded his arms. "I don't believe so. I know he was bitter because we would not let him go home, so…"

A Water didn't let him finish. "Yes, but…He grew very fond of Drip. I know because Thomas alluded to the fact that Drip, Rain, and I are orphaned. Drip must have told him because Rain and I did not. That knowledge seemed to put determination into him. He wants to help us. I'm certain." His thoughts wandered to Drip. The poor droplet was so sad. A Water wanted this all to end so Drip could once again see Thomas safe and sound. It pained him to see Drip so upset.

"Hope so." The captain rose and placed the book back on the shelf. "Let's just hope he doesn't break under whatever the flames do to him."

~~~

Thomas sank down in despair. He had been so close to finding the key. If only he hadn't knocked the armor over. Maybe he still would be free. He looked around the room the guard had placed him in. Sure enough, they had put him in solitary confinement. It made sense, this way he could not plan an escape with the lightning bolts. He was on his own now. The only light came from a small air hole in the ceiling. Thomas was grateful for the little air he got although it wasn't enough to keep the room from getting stuffy. Instead of brick, the walls of this room were made of hard-packed dirt. The floor too was dirt. He had to think of some way to get out of here. This afternoon he was supposed to appear before the king to give him his decision on whether or not he would help them destroy Rainland. Who knew what the king would do if he refused? Trying not to think about that, Thomas set about looking for any weaknesses in the walls and floor of his small prison. Everything seemed well packed. How would he find a way out?

"Hey," came a hoarse whisper. Thomas spun around. One of the flame guards he had seen in the armory was standing there with a bowl. No doubt it contained his breakfast. "Trying to get out, huh?" Thomas' heart started to pound. He had been caught trying to find a way out. "Don't worry, I won't tell." The flame gave him a smile. He opened the door and entered the small room. Setting the food down, he sat down across from Thomas. Thomas stared at the food. Several waffles with apple sauce sat there, inviting him to take a bite. The flame laughed at the shocked look on Thomas' face. "I don't like the king's cruelty. I thought I'd share my breakfast with you. You'll need strength if you are ever going to get out of here."

"Y-you're not against me?" Thomas stared at the flame in disbelief. He must be the one who had expressed displeasure at seeing the prisoners so sad.

"Nope, I like you. The king is cruel. This isn't *his* land. It belongs to the lightning. It was wrong of him to take it and also wrong of him to attack Rainland."

Thomas chewed his waffles as he tried to digest this new information. There was someone on his side in this awful place. This brought a new measure of comfort to him. Although one on his side wouldn't do a whole lot of good, it was far better than being the only one.

"Sorry, I forgot to introduce myself." The flame looked a little embarrassed. "My name is Flicker."

"It's nice to meet you, Flicker," Thomas replied, finishing his waffles. "I only wish we could have met under better circumstances."

"So do I," Flicker replied, rising to his feet. "Now we must hurry before the others find us. I am being closely watched for signs of treachery." He took out his knife and began scraping the floor. Thomas' eyes grew wide as a small metal square appeared beneath the dirt. Was this guard finding a way for him to escape? Could this be real or was he merely dreaming?

"Flicker! What's taking you so long?" a voice barked. "You should be feeding the lightning by now. It is growing late." Flicker frantically scraped away the remaining dirt, revealing a trap door.

"Hurry," he whispered, lifting the door. "You haven't much time. They don't know about this secret tunnel. I will cover it best I can once you are down."

Thomas looked through the door at the rough ground that sloped downward from the door. He would have to slide down. He hoped he would fit through. He looked at Flicker. "Thanks."

Flicker smiled in response. "Just get down there. We have no more time." Thomas could hear the approaching guard's footsteps drawing nearer every second.

Once Thomas was all the way through the hole, Flicker shut the door. Thomas could hear him frantically covering the door with dirt. He hoped that the other guard would not become suspicious when he found the loose dirt.

"What are you doing? Where is the boy?" came a thundering voice. Thomas cringed. Flicker was caught.

"He got away," came Flicker's response.

"Got away? GOT AWAY?" the other guard roared. "WHAT DO YOU MEAN, GOT AWAY?" That was the last Thomas heard as he scrambled down the tunnel. Where he was and where he was headed, he didn't know. All he cared about now was getting as far as possible from the door. The guard might become suspicious and find the door. Thomas didn't want to be anywhere near it when he did.

Chapter Twelve

"How did the prisoner get away?" questioned the flame king. "That room is very secure, I checked it myself."

The king's words sent prickles that spiraled down Flicker's spine. Did he know what he had done? He couldn't know about the secret passage, or could he? Panic surged through his stomach, making him feel like someone was flipping pancakes inside him. He must stall for time. Darting his eyes around the room he stammered, "H-he g-got away."

"I KNOW he got away," the king thundered, rising from his throne. "I asked you HOW he got out. Now answer me or I will imprison you."

Flicker faltered under his intense stare. He knew he would imprison him if he did answer. He would not take too kindly to one of his guards assisting in a prisoner's escape. If he remained quiet, maybe the king would be lighter on him. That was a big if. King Ignatius was not known for showing mercy.

The silence was deafening as he stood there aware of the king's presence growing nearer and nearer by the second. He could not look the king in the eye. He would see his weakness and no guard was supposed to show weakness.

The king's shadow fell over him. "Take him to the tower and don't give him any food. We will see if he can hold up now." The king returned to his throne.

Flicker stumbled as the guard in charge of him shoved him along. The tower. That was the one place a prisoner dreaded most. It was to be avoided at all costs. Maximum security. Flicker shook his head. He never imagined being a prisoner under these circumstances. Many times he had taken wayward flames and lightning bolts to the tower. It was more like a torture chamber than a prison. The door, walls, ceiling, and floor were made of solid iron. A special gas that caused flames to burn without light was injected into the chamber. Not one bit of light pierced the darkness once the door was closed.

The guard tightened his grip on Flicker's shoulder as he opened the tower door. He could tell there was no way he could escape. Hopefully Thomas was long gone. No doubt the king would send someone to investigate the cell he had been in. Once they started a search, they would be sure to find the secret door. The loose dirt would give it away.

The guard pushed Flicker up against the cold wall and tied his bound wrists to a small bar protruding from the wall. This would prevent him from sitting when he became tired. "The sooner you talk, the sooner you will feel better," the guard hissed in his ear. "I will be back tonight to see if you are ready to talk. If we find out first, you shall have no mercy." With that, the guard slipped out the door. The heavy door swung closed with a resounding click, plunging the room into darkness.

～～～

Thomas was completely disoriented. Where exactly might he be? He had been walking down the corridor for what seemed like hours. What had happened to Flicker? The question nagged the back of his mind. He could be suffering right now for helping him escape. Thomas grimaced. He didn't want anything to happen to Flicker on account of him. Several times the thought crossed his mind to go back and help Flicker, but he knew that it would most likely end in both of them suffering. Flicker would not want that.

Thomas sighed. The tunnel widened into a larger chamber. The dirt floor did not appear as though it had been disturbed in a long time. Old torches were attached to the walls near the ceiling. A small amount of light seeped through a crack along one side of the ceiling. The light must be coming from the lava chamber. Thomas felt the wall. It was warm. That had to be it. He must be making a circle around the lava. Now he had an idea where he was. He hadn't left the volcano.

Turning his eyes to the other side of the chamber, he noticed a door set back in the wall. *I wonder where that leads.* The door was secured with a strange looking combination lock. Instead of using numbers, this lock needed a code in letters. If only he knew what they were. The door was dusty. A small board was stuck in two clamps on the door. Thomas grasped the board and pulled it out. There was writing on the back! Thomas stared at it. It was written in some code. It read, "Nehw eh semoc eh swonk sih eman eh si a nos fo nam." What could these words mean? It must be the answer to unlocking the door.

Thomas pondered the words, trying to decipher them. Were they in a different language? Running his fingers over the letters, he thought back to the secret code book he had gotten for his birthday. What were some of the tricks? Maybe he should switch the first and last letters of each word. After trying that with the first word, it became obvious this was not the method used. Maybe they were scrambled. He looked at the first word. What word could he make out of n-e-h-w? "H-e-n-...w-e-n..." Wen? What was a wen? "That's it! W-h-e-n!" Thomas was excited. The words were written backwards. Slowly, he sounded out each word from back to front. The message read, "When he comes he knows his name he is a son of man." Frowning, he placed the board on the ground and sat down. Now what did that mean? It sounded like some sort of riddle. Son of man must be a human. What human was supposed to come here?

Thomas sprang to his feet. He was a human who had come. Did it mean him? How would whoever had written this have known he would be here? A cold eerie feeling washed over him. This was getting really weird. He put his hand on the keypad. He had to know if this was really meant for him. Hands shaking with excitement, Thomas punched in T-H-O-M-A-S and pulled on the door. Nothing. Well, so much for that. Thomas flopped back down on the ground with a sigh. He wanted so much to figure out the combination. After working to figure out the code, it seemed such a pity he could not use it.

After a lot of thinking, Thomas decided to try both his first and last names. Maybe that would work. He rose and punched T-H-O-M-A-S W-O-R-T-H-E-R into the keypad. Still nothing. Maybe he needed his middle name. Starting over he added, "Samuel" between "Thomas" and "Worther." The lock gave way. It worked! Thomas was dumbfounded. Whoever had locked this door knew that he was coming.

The hinges on the door creaked and groaned as he pushed it open. A massive corridor stretched out in front of him. Thousands of glowing rocks dotted the dirt walls, illuminating the path almost as well as if the sun were shining through a window. Thomas looked in amazement. Momentarily forgetting his excitement, his mind wandered back to the guards. Would they come looking for him? Replacing the board with the code, he closed the door, causing it to re-lock. Now he should be safe. The guards would never figure out the code.

After walking down the corridor several hundred yards, Thomas stopped in front of a crevice in the wall. What might it be hiding? Reaching inside, he felt a large object. Grasping it with his fingers, he tugged until it came free. It was a large leather-bound book. Sitting down, Thomas opened to a worn page. This appeared to be some sort of journal.

It is well past the time I ought to retire to my bedchamber but I must record this important information. One never knows when we may have need of it. Hopefully, no trouble ever befalls us, but if it does, we shall have a record of how things ought to be. At the beginning of the empire of Eldur, King Donder the 1st laid out the rules by which we are to be governed. Only descendants from his lightning family shall be heirs to the throne. Each heir to the throne shall be named Donder. At all times there shall be a King Donder on the throne as long as he is at least ten years of age. While this may sound quite selfish and potentially tyrannical, having only his descendants on the throne, it is in fact quite sacrificial. The king must protect his subjects with utmost humility and patience. He must be willing to sacrifice himself for the good of his people. This means that if an attack is to take place, he will be defending on the front lines with those of lowest rank. He is not, under any circumstance, to use his power at the expense of his subjects.

Thomas looked up from the page. This was fascinating! Was Donder one of the kings? He must be! But why hadn't he told him? Maybe he had to keep it a secret. Who had written this book? Thomas flipped to the front. A name had been written in the front, but it appeared to be in a different language. That was strange. Oh, well. Eager to read more, Thomas flipped to another page.

Flames have invaded our land. We shall soon be overtaken. I must write this quickly and hide it for we have not much time. The flames will use their power to make us lightning bolts attack Rainland. This is a most dreadful time in our history. They shall think of us as breaking our word. If only we had the power not to attack. There is talk of a boy who shall come and free us. When he comes the throne shall be restored to its rightful king and we shall once again be at peace with Rainland. The boy's name is Thomas Samuel Worther.

Thomas stared at the page. Here was his name printed in this diary from the time of the flame invasion. He couldn't believe it. What had made them think he could help them? Where had they gotten the idea?

> *Time is running short. As king, I must go defend my people. I have padlocked the door. The combination is the boy's full name. I am leaving a coded message in case he comes to this door. It reads, 'When he comes he knows his name he is a son of man.' I have written each word backward in an attempt to keep our enemies from entering this tunnel. This tunnel is the key to our eventual escape once the boy arrives. I have hidden the "special key" in the armory. It unlocks the door to our freedom at the very end of this tunnel. For now, it is safest if only I know where this key is hidden. That way the flames will not be able to get any information from the others as to its whereabouts. I have hidden it under a floorboard beneath the trunk. I made a decoy in the trunk to throw off our enemies. It is a piece of chewing gum nestled under a layer of fabric. I must go now. Donder the 15th.*

So that was why the gum was in the trunk! He had been so close to the key. Now Thomas wanted to get back into the armory to retrieve the key. They had to get out of here. Thomas flipped through the rest of the pages. They were all blank. Apparently no one had been in this tunnel since the flames had taken over. Thomas was now certain that the Donder he knew was the same Donder who wrote this diary. That is how he knew that the key was in the armory. He must not have been comfortable telling him the exact whereabouts since there were so many other lightning bolts present.

Chapter Thirteen

"I will not tell you how he got out." Flicker had been summoned to the throne room in an attempt to get information out of him.

"So, you helped him." The king rose from his throne and waved for his guards. "Flash and Crackle, lock him up and don't give him any food. Once you have him secured, I want you to go investigate the room we had the boy in. Comb it for any clues to his escape."

"Yes, your majesty." Both guards bowed before turning to Flicker. They both gave him a piercing stare.

"I thought you were getting too soft with the boy," Flash hissed, dragging him by his arm.

A sinking feeling dropped from Flicker's chest to his toes. They couldn't miss the disturbed ground in the cell. They would find the trap door. Had Thomas been able to get out? Flicker hoped his suffering was not in vain.

～

"What's this?" Crackle bent down to look at the floor of the cell that had held Thomas. He ran his fingers through the loose dirt. "It looks like someone was digging here."

Flash turned toward Crackle, his eyebrows raised. "That was hard-packed dirt when I brought the boy here." Extracting a knife from his pocket, he knelt on the floor and began scraping the loose dirt away. "Metal?" More and more of the trap door slowly appeared as he scraped away.

"Well?" Crackle looked at Flash. The entire door was now uncovered.

"We must find Thomas." Flash wedged his fingers under the edge of the door and slowly pulled it toward him. "How did Flicker know this was here? How long has he been on the lightnings' side?"

"Who knows," Crackle replied in disgust. "How could he betray us like this?"

The two flames entered the tunnel. After what seemed like an hour, Flash began to lose his patience. "How long are we going to continue? He must be long gone by now. This is a wild goose chase!" He kicked the dirt floor in frustration.

"Do you want to report to the king without finding him?" Crackle asked. Both of them knew that a failed mission would not bring the king's blessing. It was humiliating to admit defeat.

Trudging on, the two guards reached the secret door. "It's locked." Flash was disgusted. "We haven't found him. He can't be in here."

"Wait." Crackle grabbed the board from the door. "He must have figured out how to get in the tunnel. This looks like some sort of code."

Flash looked over Crackle's shoulder. "That looks like gibberish. Come on, we're wasting our time. I'm going back."

"Suit yourself. I'll get all the credit for finding him." Crackle gave him a smug smile.

Flash turned back and slumped to the floor in a huff. "We're in this together. I get no less credit than you!" he shot back.

Crackle tried every possibility he could think of but he still could not crack the code. "Just give up," Flash complained.

"We'll not give up." Crackle had a determined look on his face. "I will take this plaque to the king. Maybe he can decipher it."

"*We* will." Flash leapt to his feet, eyes flashing. "You will not get all the credit for this."

"Calm down and stop being so testy." The guards made their way back toward the trap door with the board.

Chapter Fourteen

Thomas closed the book and carefully returned it to the crevice in the wall. He must get to the key. Hopefully, he could stay out of sight this time. Opening the door, he noticed the missing board. Heart pounding, he looked around. Someone had been here while he was reading. Whoever it was seemed to be gone, but he couldn't know for sure. Thomas decided he must exercise extreme caution. He could not fail this mission. The future of two lands and his own rested on his shoulders. With a firm tug, he re-secured the door. Now, if someone came back he or she would need the code to enter. Thomas was confident that the flames would not guess the code. They only had first names. They would not likely know about middle and last names.

Thomas made his way back down the tunnel with great caution. Stopping every so often, he listened for signs of anyone else. When he was about a hundred yards from the trap door he stopped. Had he heard voices?

"I can't wait to show this code to the king," he heard. Thomas sucked in his breath. A guard! Flattening himself against the wall, he listened. "Now Flicker will really be punished." Evil laughter followed and the footsteps grew fainter.

Thomas gasped. Flicker! He had to get to the key. The sooner this was over, the better for Flicker. If he could get the lightning out of here, Donder would figure out how to rescue Flicker. Thomas was certain he would help.

~~~

This must be the right board. Thomas looked around the armory. So far he had not run into any guards. How could he lift this floorboard? A hammer would be perfect, but there weren't any hammers in sight. The armor! A loose piece of armor from the suits he had knocked over was lying on the floor. Grabbing it, he wedged the corner under the edge of the board. The board creaked as Thomas worked on getting the piece of metal underneath it. It was coming. Pushing with all his might, Thomas jammed the piece of metal under the board and lifted. There it was. Excitement built inside him as he closed his fingers around the key. Finally he had it. Now to get out of here and open the door at the end of the secret tunnel. He must tell Donder so he and the others could prepare their escape. No guards appeared to be in the hall. Thomas quietly walked along the hall that led to the dungeon. All the lightning bolts were sound asleep. The bricks Thomas had removed from the wall were back in place.

"Donder," he whispered.

Donder's eyes popped open. "Who's there?" He looked around wildly as if he expected to be in some sort of danger.

"It's okay," Thomas assured him. "It is me, Thomas. I have the key."

Donder's eyes grew large. "You found it!"

Thomas pressed his face against the bars. "I also found the book in the tunnel. We've got to get out of here.

Nodding, Donder moved closer to the door. "Be careful, they know about the tunnel. They have been trying to get me to tell them the combination. I sent them on a wild goose chase that might buy us some time. Once you get out, you can go over to the main entrance and get the master key. That will get us out of here. Throw it down our hole and wait in the tunnel."

Thomas nodded. This sounded like a dangerous mission. "I hope to be back before dawn."

Thomas scurried down the hall and back through the trapdoor. He didn't stop running until he reached the door to the secret tunnel. As soon as he had punched his name into the padlock, he pushed the door open. He made it without spotting any guards on the way. The door clicked behind him, locking out anyone who might try to follow. Safe! Thomas crumpled onto the floor, exhausted. His breath came out short and ragged from all the running. Looking ahead he could see the outline of the door. The door to freedom. *I must go on.* Every bone in his body protested, but Thomas knew he had to keep going.

Once he got the key to the lightning and he found a good hiding place, he could rest. Until then, he had to keep going. The door at the end of the tunnel looked very much like the other door with the code. Why had one been set to a code and the other one a key? Thomas inserted the key in the door and turned. The clear night sky greeted him along with a cool breeze coming from the ocean. The dark outline of Rainland was visible in the sky. Thomas wondered if the captain and A Water were still standing watch. Had they given up on him? Did they think he was even alive? What about Drip? Sadness washed over Thomas at the memory of Drip's sad face when he had expressed his displeasure about the idea of helping them.

Well, it wouldn't do to think of such things now. He was on a mission and he wasn't about to let failure be the outcome. Hugging the wall of the volcano, Thomas began making his way toward the main entrance. A strange plant with very large leaves grew along the base of the volcano. Thomas was thankful for their cover. It would be much easier to stay out of sight this way.

The closer Thomas got, the faster his heart beat. Two flame guards were stationed directly in front of the main entrance. Where were the keys kept? His eyes traveled around the door frame until they landed on a ring partially hidden by a small plant. The keys! They had to be the keys. Thomas selected a large rock from near his feet and hurled it as far as he could. It crashed through the brush growing near the water's edge.

"What was that?" one guard asked. "Intruders!" Instinctively, he took off to investigate. The other guard followed right on his heels. Just what Thomas had wanted. Now he could get to the ring of keys. Thomas dashed forward. He was right. They were the keys. Grabbing them, he dashed away from the entrance.

"The boy!"

Oh, no. One of the guards had seen him!

"After him!" the other guard shouted. "He has the keys!"

Thomas ran as fast as he possibly could. He couldn't remember ever running this fast in his life. But then, he never had a need to. While Thomas was fast, the flames were faster. They were quickly closing in on him. The hole that led to the lightning was just ahead. Could he make it? His lungs burned with each deep breath. Looking over his shoulder he saw to his horror one of the guards reaching out, about to grab his leg. If he dove, maybe he could drop the keys into the hole before he got caught. He could not let them get the keys. Launching himself into a dive, Thomas sailed through the air. The keys left his fingers the moment his hand reached the edge of the hole. Instead of stopping as planned, his momentum carried him directly over the hole. Thomas desperately tried to stop himself but it was no use. His dive took him head first through the hole. Hundreds of lightning bolts slept in a pile directly below him. The ground rushed at him with great speed. "Donder!"

Donder looked up with a shocked look on his face as Thomas tumbled into a pile of lightning bolts. "The keys," Thomas gasped.

Donder scooped up the keys and began frantically trying each one in the lock. "Everyone prepare to follow me. It won't take the guards long to get in and inform all the other guards. Pretty soon we are going to have a whole group of them hot on our heels."

Thomas breathed a sigh of relief when the door finally opened. Now the tunnel. They must make it to the tunnel. Donder led everyone down the hall and through the trap door, which slowed them down considerably. To Thomas, it seemed to take forever for all the lightning bolts to pass through the small metal door. Just as the last bolt was slipping through the trap door, Thomas heard a shout. "The trap door, after them!"

"Run!" Thomas shouted. "They are coming after us!"

Donder already had the door to the secret tunnel open when Thomas reached it. A guard was closing in on them rapidly. Everyone was in a state of panic as the lightning bolts frantically pushed their way through the door. Thomas' heart sank as the guard reached out and grabbed one of the lightning bolts. Donder hesitated at the door. Was he going to get himself captured too? Thomas held his breath.

"Go, go, and don't turn back. It won't do either of us any good." The lightning bolt struggled in his captor's arms.

Donder nodded sadly. "We'll do our best to rescue you!" he called, before securing the door behind him.

"You won't succeed!" the guard called through the locked door.

~~~

They had done it. They had gotten out of the volcano. Well, almost anyway. The fact that Flicker and one of the lightning bolts were being held as prisoners dampened everyone's excitement at finally being free. Thomas shivered in the cool night breeze. "Now what?" They were all lined up on the beach directly under Rainland.

"I will try to ask for peace," Donder replied with calm in his eyes. "They will send someone out soon I am sure. They will likely try to make a deal concerning the release of the lightning bolt they captured."

Thomas wasn't sure how he could appear so unrattled after everything they had been through. In a few minutes a flame guard emerged, holding a white flag, and made his way toward them. A lightning bolt went out to meet him. Thomas watched the expression on the bolt's face for clues to the direction of the conversation. His grim expression told Thomas the news was not going to be in their favor. Turning, the lightning bolt approached Donder. Bowing low, he spoke, "Your majesty, the guard wishes to speak with you."

"Very well, Strike." Donder slowly made his way to the flame. Thomas was dying to know what they were saying. Unlike Strike, Donder's face was expressionless. What were the flames asking of them? Were they going to keep the prisoners safe? After a few minutes the flame returned to the volcano. Donder turned to Thomas and the rest of the lightning bolts. "They said they would throw the prisoners in the lava. The only way they will release them is if I take their place. I have agreed to let them throw me in the lava in place of the lightning bolt and the flame, who they told me, betrayed them and helped Thomas escape."

Everyone gasped. "No!" Thomas shouted.

Donder turned to Thomas with a soft gaze. "Thomas, I must. I am the king. You read the book. The king must be willing to sacrifice himself for his subjects. You are to lead the people now. I have confidence you can do it." He patted Thomas on the shoulder.

Presently, the flame guard returned with the prisoners. Releasing them, he grabbed Donder and bound his hands and feet. "We've got your leader. Soon we will have you!" His evil laugh reverberated through the air, sending shivers down Thomas' spine. "You can never stand without him." The flame paused, staring directly at Thomas. To Thomas, it felt as though the flame's eyes were boring holes right through him. "You may *think* you are a leader, but you are just a boy. Don't even think of peace, we are going to *defeat* you." With that, the guard turned and disappeared into the volcano.

Donder was gone. The weight of the loss crushed Thomas. It felt as though a colossal rock was expanding in his throat. One look at the rest and Thomas could tell they felt the same way. They had lost their leader and king.

Flicker approached Thomas. "I'm at your service."

"Th-thanks," Thomas stammered. "We'll be glad of your help." Thomas knew they had to be ready. The flames were probably preparing to attack. It wouldn't take them long.

A deep rumble sounded from the depths of Eldur. Thomas prepared himself. They were coming. Thousands upon thousands of flames poured out of the volcano. Where had they all come from? He hadn't been expecting so many. Thomas braced himself as the flames rushed them.

The next minute they were a tangle of flames and lightning bolts. Thomas struggled hard to keep himself from being thrown to the ground as the flames started tackling everyone who was not on their side. How were they going to make it? They were far outnumbered. Grunts and groans filled the air as lightning bolt after lightning bolt was overpowered and bound hand and foot. Thomas began to panic. Too many of them were tied.

Did A Water and the captain see what was happening? Thomas took his eyes off the struggle to scan the border of Rainland. He couldn't tell if they were still in the lookout tower. A loud cry tore through the night as Thomas felt something slam into his back. He tumbled to the ground.

Struggling, he looked over his shoulder to see the evil grin of a flame. The flame held a rope in his hands. "No!" Thomas shouted, kicking his legs. He wasn't going to allow himself to be tied. "A WATER! CAPTAIN! HELP!" He kicked hard, freeing his legs from the flame's hands. Running forward, he stumbled into the water. The flame shrank back with a look of fear on his face. He was afraid of the water. The water would put them out. That was it. If they had a way to throw water on the flames, they could defeat them. Thomas stood and cupped his hands. "A WATER! CAPTAIN! WE NEED BUCKETS!"

Thomas searched the dark outline of Rainland. A Water's head appeared over the railing. "We are getting buckets, Thomas. Hang on!"

In a matter of minutes buckets by the hundreds were tossed from Rainland. They must have woken the entire country! Hundreds of raindrops were gathered at the railing to show their support of Thomas and the lightning bolts. "Everyone grab a bucket and start throwing water!" Thomas ordered. He grasped the nearest bucket and plunged it into the water. Lugging it onto the land, he threw the water at the nearest flame guard. Jumping back, the guard barely got out of the way. Small plumes of smoke curled from his legs where a few drops of water had hit him. As Thomas turned back to refill his bucket, he noticed all the lightning bolts throwing water as fast as they could.

"Fall back!" the flame king shouted above the noise. "I don't want to lose anyone!" Thomas and the lightning grabbed their buckets of water and pursued the retreating flames. The flame army was in a state of confusion, running into each other in a desperate attempt to stay away from the water. Thomas and his army chased them to the opposite shore. Now they were trapped. What would they do now? "Jump!" the king commanded. In one fluid motion, the entire flame army, including the king, jumped the gap between Eldur and the other island. Thomas watched as the flames lost their ability to talk and walk. The now inanimate flames licked up the grass until there was nothing left to burn and they burned out.

Thomas turned to the lightning bolts and Flicker. "We did it!" A loud cheer erupted from the army. They no longer had to fear the flames.

The first rays of the sun peaked over the horizon. Thomas, Flicker, and the lightning bolts set to work untying all the bolts who had been overpowered by the flames. When they were finished, Thomas looked up toward Rainland. "I will be right there. I just want to go inside for a couple minutes," he called to the raindrops.

Even with their victory, Thomas felt like they had lost. Walking to the edge of the lava chamber, he looked down into the boiling lava. Just hours before, Donder had been thrown into this angry pit. There was no sign of the king. He must have been completely swallowed up by the lava. Quiet sobs shook Thomas' shoulders.

"Why are you looking down there?" came a voice from behind him. "If you are looking for me, I'm behind you."

Thomas slowly turned. "Donder!" The king's arms were full of burn marks, but other than that, he looked to be in excellent shape. "I thought…"

Donder nodded. "It is written in the book, but you must not have read that part. The descendants of King Donder the 1st are bigger and stronger than all other lightning bolts. While most lightning bolts would be destroyed in the lava, we are not. Now, it does hurt us, but we recover. I knew that it would be painful, but, as king, I must look out for my subjects who are weaker than I. I wouldn't make a good king if I didn't." He smiled and placed his hand on Thomas' shoulder. "You are a brave boy. The others told me about the battle. I knew you could do it."

Thomas blushed. "I couldn't have done it without the others. None of us would have made it without the help of the raindrops. They gave us all the buckets."

"Yes, we are deeply indebted to Rainland. I have written a letter to their king." Donder extracted a fancy letter from his robe and held it out to Thomas. "Here, give this to the king once he returns. Now that the flames are gone, all who would like to return will soon be arriving."

"I must go then." Thomas stood. "I want to witness the reunion. Thank you for everything."

"Thank *you*," the king replied. "If there is ever anything you need, don't hesitate to call on us. You are always welcome here."

"I just might do that some time." With a wave of his hand, Thomas headed to Rainland.

Chapter Fifteen

Hundreds of raindrops were waiting to greet Thomas. A Water pushed his way through the crowd. "Thomas, I'm so glad to see you!"

Drip was trailing along right behind, an excited look on his face. "Thomas!" He ran into Thomas' arms. "I was so afraid for you! I'm glad you're safe."

Thomas smiled at him. "I'm glad we're all safe."

"We could hardly get him to eat, he was so worried," A Water said. "Captain and I began to lose hope. We thought you would never come back. Imagine our surprise when we saw the lightning on your side! What exactly happened there?"

"The history book you have is not the true history book of Eldur," Thomas began. He went on to tell the whole story about the flame invasion and how Eldur came to be.

"Wow!" A Water exclaimed when he had finished. "And here we thought we had to defeat the lightning."

"They're coming!" came a shout.

Thomas looked up to see the lost raindrops returning. It was a sight to see. All the raindrops who had ever been knocked out of the clouds were slowly rising from their various resting places and meeting in the air around Rainland. It looked like thousands of balloons had been released from the ground. It was breathtaking to watch. Thomas felt a surge of excitement. This is what he had risked his life to see. It brought tears to his eyes. One by one the raindrops landed on the deck-like floor of the cloud.

Drip scanned the crowd of newcomers. Gasping, he darted toward a regal-looking raindrop dressed in a flowing robe. This must be one of the kings of Rainland. Thomas decided the raindrop next to him must be the queen. She wore a matching robe. "Hey, buddy!" the king exclaimed, whisking Drip off his feet. "How have you been? Have your brother and sister been taking good care of you?"

A Water smiled at Thomas. "King Destin and Queen Acquanetta. Didn't know I was a prince, did you?" He winked at Thomas. Turning, he made his way over to the king and queen.

Thomas' mouth dropped open. Drip was a prince? He never would have guessed.

"Good job, Thomas!" barked a gruff voice. Thomas turned just as Captain H20 slapped him on the back. "Glad you made it."

"So am I," Thomas replied.

"So this is the young boy I've heard so much about." A large raindrop stood in front of Thomas. He was strangely familiar. Where had Thomas seen him before? "King Fontaine the fifth." He thrust his hand forward.

Thomas shook his outstretched hand. Where had he heard that name before? The picture! This was the king from many years ago who was pictured on the stairway to the room he had been staying in. "I never imagined I'd meet you."

"Nor did I think I would meet you." King Fontaine smiled.

"So how does it work now that more than one king is here?" Thomas was thinking about King Destin.

"Well, King Destin is the most recent king. He is king now. I will be happy to retire." King Fontaine smiled.

Thomas looked around. There was so much chaos. Almost everyone seemed to be welcoming someone they had lost in the attacks at the hands of the flames.

"Thomas!" King Destin was walking toward him. "Glad to meet you. A Water told me of your desire to return to your home. We have a plan. Unfortunately, we cannot use the rope in areas populated by people. We will have to wait several months until it is cold enough to snow where you live. Some volunteers will form a giant snow flake and float you back. I hope this is acceptable to you?"

"Yes, Your Majesty." Thomas didn't mind the wait now that he didn't feel like a prisoner. He had grown to like the raindrops.

~~~

Three months later, Thomas was preparing to return home. The air had grown chilly. All the raindrops were now snowflakes. This morning, Drip had come to him excited because he was a snowflake for the first time he could remember.

"Are you going away forever?" Drip asked as he watched Thomas pack a small bag.

"I don't know." Thomas hadn't thought about coming back. He didn't know if it was possible.

King Destin appeared in the doorway. "Thomas, if you ever need anything, don't hesitate to call on us. You are always welcome in Rainland."

"Thanks." Thomas looked at Drip. "Maybe I will be back." The two of them traded smiles as Thomas grabbed his pack. Climbing the stairs, he stopped to look at the drawing of King Fontaine the fifth. He thought about the first time A Water had led him down these stairs. It had been quite an adventure with many dangers. One thing was for sure, it was one adventure he would never forget.

A whole crew of snowflakes was waiting for Thomas when he emerged from the stairwell. "Ready?" one asked.

Thomas nodded. The whole population of Rainland had turned out to see him off. The snowflakes linked arms, forming a platform for Thomas. Climbing on, Thomas turned to wave at all the snowflakes. "I'd like to come back soon!" All the kings stepped forward and gave them a push. Thomas felt a rush of cold air as they began their descent. The trees and houses grew larger and larger until he was directly above his backyard. With a soft thud, Thomas landed on the snow-covered grass. He was home at last!

35884788R10073

Made in the USA
Middletown, DE
18 October 2016